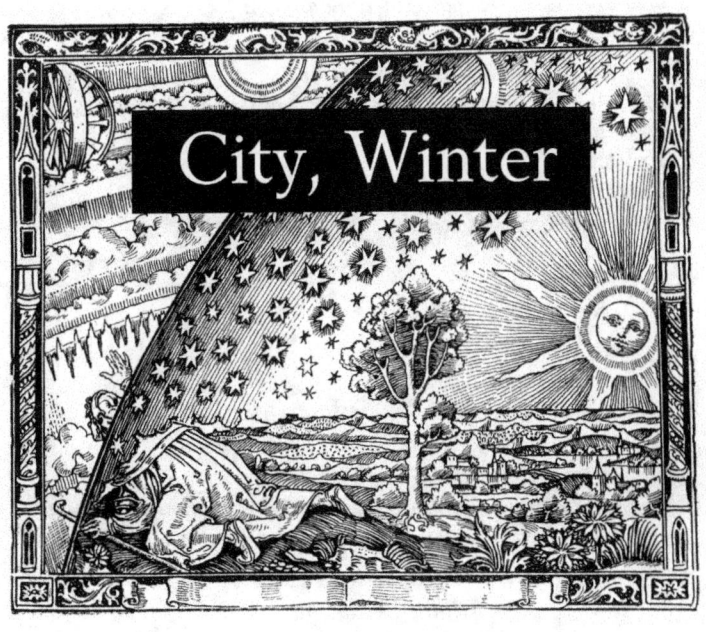

City, Winter

Robin Wyatt Dunn

By Robin Wyatt Dunn

By Robin Wyatt Dunn

SHORT STORIES
Dark is a Color of the Day

PLAYS
Last Freedom

FILMS
A Wilderness in Your Heart
Party Games
American Messenger

JOHN OTT
SAN DIEGO, CALIFORNIA
2020

ISBN - 978-1-940830-34-6
LOC - 2020942900

Cover art by Barbara Sobczyńska

for Jon Levi

Part 1

1.

I took my dog Henry for a walk down to the corner store, closed now for the storm. The city has been growing despite the cold: its fingerlike spires range so far above now in the wind they cannot be seen.

I wish the store would open: I can see the fruit rolls right on the other side of the window. So can Henry.

The wind is rising. I grin into it and watch the lights of the police cruisers fade into the snow.

"It's gonna be a long one, buddy!"

He smiles. Long ones mean lots of extra biscuits.

Henry can see things I can't. He can see a very long way, actually.

- -

I am writing a letter to my advisor. My dissertation is almost complete. *The Uses of Color in Braunschweig: Studies in Paranoia.* I know, the title is overblown. But academics love colons.

Outside the snow is covering the window. But I can see the church through the ice, blinking its light. I had volunteered to sing this season. I'm going to need a new scarf.

- -

We're singing "All of Heaven's Angels" and Angela is one of them. The priest is watching the two of us. Outside, I can hear the hail.

The color of the priest's robe is blood, to represent our savior's sacrifice. But I see it as a kind of lightning storm, rubbing underneath our clothes, raising static. Angela smiles at me and I wink at her; something I've never been able to do before.

"Are you taking the bus?" I ask her, after.

"Yes."

"Let me walk you."

"No thank you but I'll see you later," she says, waving her hand under the snow. She walks carefully over the hail balls. I watch her disappear into the white.

Braunschweig is growing, but so am I. I pay my rent; I keep my mouth shut when it counts. But what I want to know is: where are we going? What are we becoming?

2.

The fruit roll is in my hand. Jack, the owner, had given me two through the slot, though he did not want to open. He knows that Henry craves them. I hand him one and eat the other slowly, looking at my computer.

Blood and black are the two colors I've specialized in. But a particular kind of brownish-black: the color of the buildings here.

Both are about fertility: one of blood, of course, and the other is the color of rich soil. Sometimes I think the night sky is that way too: a fertile field.

\- -

I run down to the registrar in the sleet, duck under the transom and shake my pass at the secretary.

"Oi!"

"Not now Mrs. Selverson!"

Down to the library. Under the arch of Saint Pepper, his arms wide, like mine, as I display the signature on my sheet:

"He's signed!" I say to the Registrar.

"We're closed, Thomas. Come on."

"I have to file it today!"

"What is it?"

"Stamp it, stamp it, please!"

He looks at me with the long suffering bureaucrat eyes, the eyes of the priest ever since he crawled out of the ground.

"Please!"

He raises his right arm, and crosses himself.

Down, down comes the hammer. Red, red as blood.

"Thank you!"

Out, and under the transom.

"Oi!"

"I love you Mrs. Selverson!"

"You've gotten mud in the entry!"

"I promise to polish it tomorrow!"

Out into the white noise, stunning my head; I wrap the scarf around my face, and the form around my chest. The red ink will stain my shirt, but I can wear that emblem for eternity, when I am ordinated.

The white university seems to hover over the street like an angry ghost with raised arms; I dodge traffic and head under the gargoyles, across the quad, and into the seminary.

I will be a lay priest; my ordination will be simple (I could not swear to celibacy). The brothers are below, praying (and eating) but what I need is upstairs, Mr. Genevieve, O Genevieve, you ninety year old tramp!

Each step bears the marks of 900 years of feet, bent into the stone: up, up, up.

Around and around. Up into the scriptorium.

Bathed in light. The man himself is poised over his manuscript.

I bow before him in exaggeration, like a medieval supplicant (which is what I am, though these are modern times!) and he looks at me with a strange look in his eyes which I ignore.

"Sir, please. I need to file this form."

He points to the stack.

"Please, sir, if you don't mind. I need to have it filed today."

"You're late." His voice is low, like rumbling stones.

"I'm sorry."

He goes to examine the paper.

"You'll need a fine copy, for the examination. But this will be fine. Here, let me sign it."

He furrows his huge brows at my cover page.

"Colors, isn't it?"

"Yes."

"Very dangerous."

"Yes, it is."

3.

Braunschweig means "brown clan" – straight-forward enough. But "brown" only means the color post 13th century; before that it meant both "dark, dusky" and "bright," supposedly in part a reference to burnished wood. But deeper in, brown is related to *bear* and *birth*, in the root **bher*, which also means "carry," "maintain," and "take."

That clan, doin stuff. Here in the silence of the snow:

4.

I have been given an assignment to track a man.

Color comes from *kel: cover, conceal, save. Related to: helmet, hold, occult, hall, hell, cellular, cojones, and valhalla.

In concealment we desire to slip unnoticed into the general space: to be quotidian, normal.

Color is spycraft and pursuit; exile and return.

The color of the tree is very close to my building, but darker: like it is the bark that has peeled off the apartment.

It stretches over the bricks signaling some dark thing, looking for a deeper thirst that's in the sky.

"We're concerned he may harbor certain attitudes which could be unfriendly to the university," Mr. Genevieve had said.

I know the university is defended with blood;

and so have been for centuries. But where the rubber meets the road, as it were, here in my body . . . I haven't been able to bring myself to go to the address.

The dog is watching me. His color is like dirty snow. Wide brown eyes.

"I know Henry. You're not telling me anything I don't already know."

Just grit your teeth and run the gauntlet, Thomas:

5.

Thomas means "twin," to match my mind. It may also be related to *tehom*: the Deep.

I had quit smoking but I lit up and moved into the snow, looking up to say goodbye to my dog.

He barked in farewell. I stepped onto the bus platform and held on to the rail, watching the lights blur against the glass.

\- -

It was almost more silent inside the bus than outside it, its lights shuddering gently as we glided over the snow.

Through the glass, spiral edges of frost. Outside, my countrymen moved as beasts of burden under the weight of the white sky.

I arrived and got off the bus. The hiss and squeal of the hydraulics was muted under the wind, picking up now. I wrapped my scarf tighter around my neck and walked, reading the addresses.

334, 336, 340. I needed to be on the opposite side of the street.

In crossing, a woman looked up at me as though in recognition. I kept moving, up to 403, under the stern gaze of an angel in stone, and rang the buzzer for Bruno Wenclas, apartment 8.

"Yes?'

"May I come in?"

"I've been expecting you."

He buzzed the door open into the foyer. More angels, little quartz figures perched over the railing.

He appeared at the top of the stairs, a bear of a man with a black beard.

"Come up," he said. "How is our Gandalf?"

"He's fine. He's concerned about you."

"I know. I'm a traitor. Is Gandalf white or grey now?"

"He's white."

"He should be losing his memory then."

"His seems sharp as ever."

"Ha ha! Will you have some tea?"

His apartment was very neat. A large bookshelf dominated the far wall. Half-human statues perched in the corners.

"My people. I talk to them sometimes. Black or green?"

"Black."

He prepared the tea and I looked at the statues. They were very striking figures, like Roman household gods. He brought the tea and we sat around a small chest serving as a table.

His eyes were dark.

"Here, lift your tea," he said. I raised the saucer off the chest and he opened it, bringing out a book. "This was my treason," he said.

The book was handsomely produced, in fine paper, with a multi-colored abstract cover. At first I could see no title or author's name but then I saw his at the bottom in small white lettering:

bruno wenclas

"It looks nice."

The treatise inside, written in an elegant style, spelled out its premises in bold letters:

1) The City proper no longer exists.
2) We must find the real City, hidden in its bones.
3) If we do so, we will be able to escape.

"You're not a prisoner," I said.

"Our Gandalf has forgotten more than any of us knew, already. But one thing he does remember is why we came here. You know the story of our founding."

"Yes, as an acknowledgment to winter. Realizing that it would not leave us, we built it to honor Him."

"Sure, it's a ridiculous story," Wenclas said, "but in a way it's quite accurate. What do you think that means, building a city to honor winter?"

"Well, it's like a temple isn't it. Like the university. We use it to serve the public."

"No, that's quite wrong. You're very naïve, I'm sorry. You should tell Genevieve that I'll surrender to his goon squad whenever he likes. I don't want to fight. I have my work to think of."

"What happened when you tried to leave?"

"Some strange things. What do you think this winter is, Thomas?"

I realized then that he was mad. But like so many things, it depends on where you stand.

6.

Winter remains for me a divine intervention, something so deep in our culture here that we no longer think of it.

Who am I to speak of its many names here, a mere acolyte; what is it I expect to prove in my investigations? I know what we were fleeing. However strange our stories here, they are the best defense that simple people could muster.

Like the snow insulates the mind and body from the air and sky; what appears a weapon is actually a shield. Allowing us to give in to our burrowing instinct, and dig in, and learn.

Henry is dancing on his back legs, pawing my chest, and licks my face.

I give him his bone and go to the window to watch the light-men string their glowing beads over the buildings, their masks like medieval demons.

One of them peers into the window and I

wave, as he tosses another light-string down
the side of the wall, sparks in the dark.

7.

"The King has died," Mr. Genevieve announced.

"What do you mean? What king?"

Mr. Genevieve led me downstairs.

"I am sorry you never had a chance to meet him," Genevieve said, guiding me into the basement where a man lay under lights, submerged like Lenin inside a glass box.

"Who is this?"

"George VIII."

"The Eighth? I don't understand. What king?"

"If he had been living when you were to pass your exam, you would have had to swear loyalty to him. But things are changing. Our secret king is dead, and no successor has been chosen. It would seem the university is in agreement: no new monarch will be permitted. However

. . ."

The man in the box looked like a bad caricature of an Edwardian English king from a television show.

"I am forced to violate one of our department's customs because we like you, Thomas. We want you to stay. You know Shakespeare's play *Richard II*?"

"Of course."

"It encapsulates the ancient trope of the king as the land. The Fisher King is the same story. When the king is sick, the land is sick. If he had been healed, so too would the land be. You're familiar with how our City came to be encapsulated in winter?"

"As an artifact of nuclear exchange."

"To be sure. In part. Yes. What we need is this: you must proclaim the king's death. You must tell the City."

"I don't understand. We don't have a king. Who is this man? Why are you giving this job to me?"

"He's our secret king. But in death, he must become our public king. And in doing so, we could end the winter."

I laughed, despite myself. "What do you mean?"

"This proclamation will be very dangerous. No one else wants the job."

"Why?"

"This corpse keeps us safe, Thomas. If we remove that protection, other forces will grow more interested in our position here."

"I don't understand."

"You should be safe enough. But people remember the messenger, you see. The deliverer of bad news. It's possible the people will not mind; they know we have lied before. Perhaps they even forgave us."

8.

I slept with Henry on the bed that night, watching the snow fall. They say each raindrop and snowflake are the carriers of singular microorganisms; little points of congealing fluid to be boats for those germ-explorers. Seeking new life and new civilizations.

Our city was one of a few shelters from the nuclear winter; we survived better than most because of our river. It remained potable throughout the worst years. We do not have an official language; there must be a hundred spoken here at least. Why an English king? It doesn't make any sense.

Henry woofs low in his throat, a gentle scold.

- -

"I'm sorry I haven't scrubbed the floor yet Mrs. Selverson!"

"We'll find other ways to get it out of you, young man."

I smiled nervously and nodded, ducking past her through the atrium, back down to the basement.

Mr. Genevieve opened an enormous tome; a book the size of a small car.

A Renaissance-style pen and ink portrait of a younger looking version of the corpse I'd seen earlier glared out at me. Thin nose, dark beard, a lazy eye. Even in the drawing his clothes looked too tight.

"George VIII," Mr. Genevieve said in a low voice.

"What happened to the Seventh?"

"That was in England. Before the bombings."

"And you say he ruled our city?"

"Ruled? Oh no. He was our secret king. Do you know what a secret king is?"

"No."

"Well, you know what a king is."

"Yes."

"Well, a secret king is the same, just secret. Here, read."

Recollections, 15ᵗʰ August

I took an arrow in the back at Richibucto and thrust our regiment thirty miles back from the coast, watching the sky descend on us like a heavy, smothering blanket . . .

9.

. . . we were more dead than alive, at least in our minds. One should not suppose that we were so tired though, despite the fighting. We were wide awake. The coast had already vanished behind the white haze; I wouldn't see it again for twenty years.

We were plenty well equipped for winter; we had expected to be dug in on the coast for another month. But the blast changed everyone's plans.

It had other colors to it too—not just white—a kind of dark rainbow, the sort that wanted you to keep staring at it.

I felt in my pocket for my household god; he was still there, hard under my thumb.

"We're going to get mowed down," my second said to me.

We had no gear fit to survive radiation fallout, so I gave the order to dig. Small animals survive disaster all the time with just a few inches of soil between them and the world; I thought it was worth a try.

*We took the roofs off two jeeps, laid them over the hole
we'd dug, and piled soil on top of it. For breathing
holes we used the exhaust pipe. Then we huddled down
in our makeshift grave with nothing but a few lit can-
dles and protein bars and waited.*

*I found myself thinking of my first wife, who had al-
ways made the best onion soup. I can't say there's much
else good I remember about her, but the thought of the
soup was a comfort and a torture there in our hole. Our
neighbor grew her own onions, and always gave us some.
And my wife would toast little pieces of bread, and put
them in with the cheese to bake over the soup.*

*Eventually we could tell the fallout had reached us; it
had a kind of sound to it, not unlike the sound of
Saturn. The planet's rings make noise, you know, a
kind of music, audible on the electromagnetic spectrum.
I read it's caused by vibration in the rings, small mete-
orites stuck between the orbits of much larger ones. A
kind of natural record groove.*

Some of us sang songs to drown it out.

We sang 'I'm deep in the Home,' 'Russian snow' and

'Eliza's stars' maybe a thousand times that week, watching each other's eyes get slowly more crazy.

10.

The storm is coming over the air; a light rain followed by lightning.

The foremen of the skyscrapers surrender their aeyries for the evening; spreading tarps over their tools and tying their knots, and descending in the great open elevators to the earth.

I'm wet and running to the bus stop, the tattered page I stole from the library wet, with ink running, over my hand. A capital offense. Well, not really. A moral one. I felt I wanted to see it outside of the library, to test if it was real. Ancient archives must surely have been destroyed for even less logical reasons.

The blood is still on my boots. I splash into a puddle, and then another. The lights of the bus pull out of the rain and I get on and show my pass, down to the back in the damp and cold. Through the window I can see people running through the darkening storm.

The archive was of Samuel. Or perhaps, "by

right of Samuel" to use the imperial phrase. Empire itself is a mystery to me. Etymologically the word means "in preparation," but in preparation for what? What are we being prepared for? Slaughter? Or something else?

Samuel appears to be some kind of ur-king in our basement. Not George. His ancestor—or predecessor. I'm not sure they're related. How long have they been living down there?

11.

To understand Braunschweig I realized I would have to try to understand Ing.

Believe it or not, it is for him that English was named. England took its name from the Inga-vones, who worshipped a kind of Prometheus figure named Ing. He has his own rune, as well:

I can still read through the bled ink:

I'm waiting inside your arms;   the fever breaks over me
and the name of the world speaks for me, reciting my
names, in king

in king is ing

ing

12.

I've been reading too long; I apologize. It makes me a bit funny in the head.

The snow has stopped. I go outside and look at the white sky. Perhaps it holds the secret I'm looking for. For Roman augurers, all truths were literally written in the sky, in the form of birds.

There is crow watching me from the top of the building.

13.

"You must be very careful. This is propagan-da."

"Isn't that our bread and butter, magister?"

"You shame the name of our profession."

"I'm just being honest."

"Maybe the headline is too blue."

"I can change it. Simple black?"

"Yes."

OPEN FOR DISCUSSION

**Events in town, and our interpretations.
Historical relations.
Singing.**

8 o' clock at the Marble Theater

**Hosted by the Braunschweig
English Department**

"We're going to hell, aren't we?" he mutters.

"Do you believe in hell, magister?"

"It is a place in the mind."

He rests his hand on his hat, like he is afraid it might fly off. "I'm going out. See that the ink dries will you?"

"Yes."

14.

I walked through town putting up the fliers.

"So we're getting together then, eh?" a white-haired woman said to me, looking at the poster.

"Yes, ma'am."

"Time to rustle the rafters, is it?"

"Maybe!" I smiled.

"Is it about the king?"

"Yes."

15.

The eaves of the theater were the same color as the tree outside my window. The king sat in his throne on the stage, and Mr. Genevieve stood beside him, speaking into the microphone:

"His Majesty, George the Sixth."

He handed the microphone to the king.

The king raised it to his lips. He coughed, and it echoed over the auditorium.

"I've been dead; I'm sorry for that. But there's no time for that now. I must abdicate immediately! Here, take my crown, take it!"

He dropped the microphone into his lap and removed the crown from his head. Startled murmurs in the audience. He thrust it at Mr. Genevieve, who regarded it as a particularly nasty boil.

Mr. Genevieve nevertheless bent and took the thing, and placed it on his head. He raised the microphone to his lips.

"It does feel like a crown," he said. He took it back, gently, from off of his head. "But as your majesty knows, this is a democracy, and if we are really to be rid of your kingship, even in death, we must take a vote."

He raised his eyes to the audience and in his best professor's voice announced:

"Will those who favor a continuation of the monarchy, please step to your left. Those who favor its abolishment, to your right, please."

The hall of bodies parted. I was left standing in the middle. I ran to the stage to assist in the counting.

My fellow citizens stood as quiet and as solemn as though they were to be hanged, as I called out the numbers.

16.

"Who did you get to play the king?" I asked Mr. Genevieve.

"An old friend from my theater days. He still has some of that regal flair. What did you think of the vote?"

"A clear majority. I'm surprised so many people showed up, to be honest."

"You're a cynic. I mean, how do you think we will fair without our king?"

"I don't know. People seem to manage it."

Mr. Genevieve stopped in front of his apartment. Overhead, the sky promised more ice.

"I'll be needing you again soon, professor. Will you be able to help?"

"Yes, of course." He closed the door, leaving me in the cold. I wanted a cigarette but I would settle for a drink.

I sent Angela a message but received no answer. Then the Horn and Hooves beckoned, its goaty face thrust pugnaciously into the storm:

17.

People are very strange and it is no use explaining why it is they do what they do. It is hard enough to explain *what* they do, a task I realize I have already given insufficient attention to at points in this narrative. Here lies my conundrum: which details are important, and which are unimportant? And how can I know which will be such to you? The task appears impossible but, since many complete it every day, I remain steadfast in my belief that it will eventually make sense to me.

The winter is the reason for it: her healing mass. Such that it might remove from our bosom even the berry of life itself.

I have been standing outside Angela's apartment in the snow. She is not answering her phone, nor the banging I have been doing on her door. One of the neighbors has become aggravated.

"Go away, I am a professor!" I told him. Perhaps they will call the university.

I can see her face at the window, looking out.

I am ashamed to be this man below, looking at a woman I cannot have.

18.

Wenclas found me. I had been drinking, and was not able to dress properly before answering the door. Well, really he just came through it, to where I had been resting in the kitchen.

"Yes, the whiskey still remains. It's here." I raised the empty bottle.

"Time to sober you up," he said. He lifted me from under both armpits and guided me to the shower.

"Stand under there for five minutes and then I'll try one of my remedies on you."

- -

"How did you know where I lived?"

"You're in the directory."

"Right."

"Mrs. Selverson was worried about you."

"Really?"

"I believe your acquaintance made an unofficial complaint."

"I wish I never had to see her again."

"Let's go for a walk."

\- -

Some say the city is growing by itself, but this is not true. It is just that we have abandoned most notions of central planning in the erection of our skyscrapers. In many ways, they are art projects solely. Can New York or Shanghai really say theirs were any different?

We walked up the open air stairwell on the high-rise nearest my building, two blocks to the north. It stretches some forty stories above my roof, a skeleton like Ivan Denisovich's in Siberia . . . awaiting its tar paper.

We Braunschweigers pay the workers ourselves,

from taxes, but many of them devote addition-
al time to their projects. There is no deadline;
the things just keep rising into the sky.

"I have to tell you something about my work,"
Wenclas said. "Are you familiar at all with the
American government's experiments with psy-
chic manipulation?"

"No, not really."

"They weren't necessarily very good at it
from what I've read, but they tried everything.
Mind-reading has advanced quite a bit from the
old days, but it still runs up against some fundamental barriers: what, after all, is the mind?
In theory you could control a man like a machine if you stirred all the right circuits in his
brain, but in addition to the fact that it doesn't
actually work quite that way, it's not necessarily something that they want. Of course, the
Americans, per se, no longer exist. But their
experiments continue. I've received some of
their broadcasts."

"What do they say?"

"Creepy shit."

Wenclas' grin was wide and crazed. "Tell me," I said.

"They're looking for volunteers. On a whim, one night, I sent them a response. With my ham radio, you understand. But the next transmission I received wasn't through my radio. It was upstairs instead."

He pointed at his head.

The snow was falling heavier now, as we climbed. Looking down on the city it looked like a failed construction site, or an abandoned archaeological dig.

I had had some similar experiences since coming to Braunschweig, but such is the overwhelming social conditioning against revealing that you have old voices in your head that I said nothing.

Finally, I asked: "And what did they say?"

"It wasn't words. More of a feeling. And a sound. A sound like an old car, slowly revving up."

"Why are you telling me all this?"

"I thought you might understand."

"I don't think I do. But I want to. I feel like we have so little power here; that we're stuck. I want to know what's happened to us."

"Me too. The city is a big receiver, Thomas. I think it's being tuned."

19.

Color the concealer. Color a cloak of darkness. Color in shades and silks and long draughts, color in rage, heat, and on stage, brilliant, meant to conquer you, to divine you, possess and interrogate you, control the arc of your step.

It seems both Wenclas and I are working with radiation. Mine is merely the more quotidian of the two. One step up or down on the electromagnetic scale . . .

Wenclas' face seemed to shimmer in the light; like an artifact of some digital generator. Of course it was only the peculiar effect of the snow on the last of the sun's rays.

He was telling me about his ordeal: everyone had thought him mad. He almost lost his scholarship. It occurred to me that there are worse things than getting kicked out of school; but it's so easy, isn't it, to manage someone else's life for them. For myself, I could hardly imagine it. My identity has been bonded so deeply to this institution; I am a kind of slave.

Color is dangerous not because of what it conceals but because of what it reveals. Consider the lizard, who in his anxiety to expel the foreign invader with a blue stripe on his head rather than a white one (even though it was only painted there by a scientist) considers a fight to the death over the jump in the wavelength of light.

More than anything, my research has taught me that the Age of Reason is a lie. We are subject to more powerful forces than we can understand, and the nature of our inquiry is one of them. Not that I want to wallow in mere mysticism, you understand.

I want to be free.

Overhead I could see the streak of a meteor, flashing through the white sky; a sinking yellow scar. I felt vertigo for a moment; the street seemed to dance towards me, and Wenclas grabbed my shoulder.

"We'd better go," he said.

"I'm in trouble," I said.

"What is it?"

But behind him I could already see the face of the inquisitor, his blood red robes almost black in the light.

I felt Wenclas' urge to scream, but he controlled himself.

"We were just leaving," he said.

The inquisitor smiled. I had never seen the man. He looked a bit like the dead king.

"The light is beautiful this time of night. I often come up here myself," the inquisitor said. He leaned against the wall, as though he were a thief about to light a cigarette.

"Yes it is," I said.

"I think I may have made a mistake," the inquisitor said. "Bright young men like you wouldn't make such a fuss over these details; I know it's too much for you. I can see how it might have been; I was a student once myself. Now you're going to have some explaining to do."

"Really, we were just going," Wenclas said, and made to move past the inquisitor.

The inquisitor took hold of Wenclas' arm, gently.

"I'm sorry," he said. "You're both going to come with me."

His eyes were a color I've never seen. The non-color of the night after you have closed your eyes.

20.

It is said that in the beginning, the Spanish Inquisition was true to its name: they wanted only to understand what it was the people of the Iberian peninsula believed. They were curious men.

I whose curiosity is a fire have a strange respect for this origin story—even if it is not true. How strange it is to be burdened with curiosity, waiting for its birds to hatch. Making strange noises over your head, as they hunt for food. As they prepare to fly.

Bird men, beckoning to the night, to come on in, and show your face, whoever you are. . .

I am only a foolish Romantic. But still I can hear the sounds.

I have been granted one phone call. I thought to call Angela but thought better of it. Instead I called my uncle Martin.

"Yes? Hello?"

"I'm in jail Martin. Can you bail me out?"

21.

I who have now been changed—probably destroyed—still must document the process, if not for historical reasons than simply for my own vanity. I want to know and remember how it was that I became a prisoner of the state.

I've leapt ahead and must apologize. I have never been very good at telling stories in a straight line. There is something about stories which resist straightness in my opinion.

I spent two years in prison at Jahed El-Bashon, otherwise known as Chesterfield. My uncle did attempt to help me, but things were too far gone for that. It continues to be strange to me—perhaps you have lived through something similar—that one can be raised comfortably in a society and only discover quite late in life that all of its origins are lies, and that, moreover, it is actively preying on you. Some never have to face such horrors, either because they were fortunate to grow up permanently sheltered, or because they never wanted to know anything else.

I wanted to know and so I did. and the changes this wrought are, I suppose, the subject of
this narrative. How did my city come to subdue
me? It came first in the colors of the Inquiry to
which I was set as a prisoner:

Part 2

22.

The inquisitor made a display of colors:

"We'd like you to consider the alteration of the sequence, Thomas. Please watch again."

The orders of the medieval dance—inscribing, not unlike the Western American square dance, both the peasant village phenomena of separation and reunion of men and women but also the hierarchy of the social classes and interreliance—struck over the floor in history the arch like Greek and Roman combat its phalanx, centered and moored but prepared to *launch*:

Hieram, the man who had arrested me, set to the floor the bloody colored hem of his robe and his brethren in this dance: well.

Again I have to backtrack.

They turned me in to a kind of fashion consultant. They used my dissertation against me. But also: they showed me just what it was I had done.

I'm tempted to claim slaves cannot again act against their masters, however often they rise in insurrection. Perhaps French echoes this conundrum, since its everyday *sortir* echoes the Latin *in surgo*—I arise—these continual leave-takings and return, however couched in messianic absolutist terms. All of this is to say: I was overwhelmed. I was not myself.

A city which had appeared to me to be glum and quotidian was revealed to be the masterwork of deception set upon by an (avowedly) ancient cult. Ordered and bent to order my will; to convert me.

Did Rome really leave Etrusca behind? Or Etrusca its Anatolia? Rather it seems they merely further eddy the waters, which flow further, deeper, in the same direction, as the earlier conqueror:

Is it wise then, for me to admit I am conquered? Even to express some joy in this? It cannot be; yet I still am tempted to make the claim.

Suddenly I am filled with urgency—am I running out of time? There is so much I want to say and so little time in which to do it—whatever truth I stumble on must be fleeting, yet it is my longing for it to be eternal; I am ashamed.

Just tell the story, Thomas. It will be all right.

Well: I was captured, as I said. I was made to watch the procession.

Consider Prokofiev's famous dance of the Montagues and Capulets:

That square dance. The square is no accident, you understand. Even as the hexagon that spins atop our sun's sixth planet is no accident, and its accompanying cultic ornaments, well known to students of such things: the Qaaba, and the phylacteries.

In ordinating procession—like the electromagnetic spectrum, you see—Hieram and his inquisitors prepared their dance in red:

23.

But it was also yellow.

I am tempted again to skip this part of my narrative altogether: it seems so unbelievable. Yet my research has led me to conclude this is a repeating feature of the mind control cults common, at least throughout the late 20th and early 21st century cults in North America: kid-napping, followed by extraordinary events that no other witness would believe. In this way the cult protects itself.

I should have remained at the edges, you see. And, in actuality, it may be that I have. But I took a trip towards the center, on one of those random eddies which spiral out towards the bank, and came into the stream:

Bodies of red and yellow swarmed across the palazzo, with such force it left me wide eyed. They moved in contrapuntal lines, like sashes across the chest, the priest alternately ascend-ing and descending the ornamental stairways to denote a swirling mobius strip.

"Is the position of the curve of bodies, arced back in on themselves, fundamental to the structure of the human race, or is it something we impose, would you say?" Hieram whispered in my ear.

"A feedback loop," I mumbled. I know I had been drugged.

"But a feedback loop from what to what?"

"Give me another hit, doc."

24.

The cell is quite beautiful; even comfortable, in a way. I am afforded a stunning view of the river, frozen solid now for 75 years, and its surrounding banks, gleaming white. Only a few trees poke their heads through the freeze, old men unable to help themselves, stubborn, hunched alone.

Every morning I rise late, perform my ablutions in the wash basin, and sit down with the pen and paper they have provided to write this narrative. It is a great joy to me, that I who have now had so many other things denied me, should be permitted still this excess: to labor in the intellectual quarter, however inadequately, to try and understand what has happened to me and my city.

"Do you need anything?" my gaoler asks at the door. She is quite pretty.

"No, thank you. Well, some crackers, if you can spare them."

She slipped a packet under the door and I pushed them whole into my mouth, to let them dissolve on my tongue as I watched the white sky dissolve into faint blue under the rising sun.

I am going to escape.

25.

Action. The thing that eluded Hamlet has found me, carrying a briefcase into the prison psychiatrist's office, under the terrible yellow glow of the fluorescent lamps.

It's funny; I'm always trying to get further away from what's happened, or closer in, but it doesn't really matter: it keep revolving around me, sunning me in space to inform me as to what is happening; what I should say next.

I understand; you only want to know what happened, and this is something I am grateful for, and I share your desire. In pursuit of it I must breaking even further the ordered series of events.

The man gave me some pills, watching me carefully with his yellow eyes, like I was wasting his time, and I handed him his prop from out of my briefcase: a silver blue frog, gleaming evilly in the flat fluorescents.

"What's this?"

"You're to play the frog. The warden says it's okay."

"What?"

"You're going to be in a play."

Never complain, never explain, yet I must do both. You're going to be in a play and what a damned sight it is; how disgusting and human and obscene; inescapable but with an end, and the reason, gracious guest:

What were we doing. Who moved us left and right, shucking us out of our cocoon to place us up in our esconcements, lion to Thebes, set to announce the coming of the kingdom, and the coming of its end, all here in the hour, for our voice, being holy, trickles electric over all the surfaces of the heavens and over the earth, washing our arms and faces in its illimitable embrace, honest workmen endowed with certain inalienable rights, none of them being life, liberty, property or the pursuit of happiness but only our incorruptible hornswoggle stubborn mule head, bent into the wind and insisting on announcing:

"Ladies and gentlemen"

"Damas y cabballeros"

Good ladies and gentle men, unwrought and undeserved, please stay a while, for our show, the last show on earth, to greet us deep and hard in the night where we have set our camp, so to see just who it is we are:

26.

Lights; not many. It's dark. Can barely see the stage (paid for by tax money). Where is my mark?

What secrets exist between men and women, and why are they diminished in the speaking of them?

I doesn't matter, Thomas. Say your lines.

"Out of the darkness, poetry. And out of the poetry, music."

The violinist, the prettiest redhead you have ever seen, starts up in the rafters.

"I wish I could tell you, ladies and gentlemen, that it's going to be all right. But it isn't."

Cue cutthroat, swaggering into the light and crouching by the wall, picking his fingernails. Over the other side of it the blank and baleful face of Gone Henry rises, announcing:

"Do you think you'll kill him yourself?"

"No, I want you to do it Henry. All right?"

"All right." His voice is like a sound emerging from deep water.

"You have to plant it hard in his chest, right into his heart." He holds the dagger out to Gone Henry. "All right?"

"What will you do?"

"I'll be watching. Making sure only the right people see."

I open my mouth, in my black: "The death of the warden. The end of the world."

The sirens begin; and the violinist turns on her amplifier; the wailing is joined by her frenzied scraping.

The warden descends on the rope, vomiting brightly colored blood over the stage; I hold his hands behind his back as he lands, and

Gone Henry and the cutthroat crouch before him like supplicants. Then Henry rises, and thrusts the dagger into his heart.

We cue the strobe, itself a kind of stiletto, and the gore is seared into people's eyes.

27.

I thrust my fist into the psychiatrist's face and was amazed with joy as bright blood spurted from his nose. The week I spent in solitary was worth that transcendent moment.

"Why are you in here, Thomas?"

"Not doing what I was told."

"Why's that?"

"Can't bear it anymore, that's all."

"Can't bear what?"

"The world."

28.

Medication, it must be remembered, is a bastardization of medicine, a thing which was never in its origin purely chemical. Music is a form of medicine; dance and song, along with herbs. Lab-bred chemicals made from herbs are all right, if you go in for that sort of thing; but on their own they can never be medicine.

Medicine means healing; and healing is not about things.

This did not matter to the authorities of Braunschweig, however, and I was forced to imbibe all manner of chemical agents during my extended stay at Jahed El-Bashon. Although their chief purpose is to make inmates more tractable (Thorazine was originally marketed in the 20th Century, for instance, for its ability to "Remove Senile Agitation!"), for me their effect has been to deepen my resolve. Under the sweaty barrier of their mists, it is easy to see how weak they are. How little they understand. How far they have come from the mission of the university.

Although it is equally likely I failed to understand what it is the university means. In my youth I had thought, and was so taught, that it celebrated "a universe of ideas," the golden panoply of human knowledge. But its etymology—"out of many, one"—suggests a more federalizing goal. University as governor.

We are being pulled apart; but I am separating myself from the 'we' . . .

29.

One underappreciated aspect of imprisonment is how you are a source of amusement to your captors. And, contrary to my expectations, this is not necessarily a cruel or exploitative mechanism. Nor can I dismiss it simply as Stockholm Syndrome. It has something to do with the nature of entertainment: the captive audience. Prisoners understand well how it is just as easy to see the state as your captive, forced as they are to take elaborate measures to reduce you to a state of fear, hopelessness and slavery.

"Go on, give me a poke at that robe," I tell the inquisitor, and to my surprise, he smiles, and offers the edge of the fabric to me.

I rub it between my fingers. "Hot damn, it's good enough to put a baby to sleep on."

He laughs, a rich musical thing. In my work as an educator, in what now seems to me to be a former life, I noted how young people often adopt the jester's hat when they do not know the answer; so too for me now.

"Do you let your wife touch this thing?"

He smiled but did not answer. He was one of Hieram's subordinates: not as smart but not as kind either. I was not looking forward to his questions.

30.

One can surmise any man is made of many
shapes; hexagons and strange polyhedrons
colliding. We have no decision over their shape,
nor their origin or destination. We can only
nudge the things up these Sisyphean slopes,
grinning in the heat.

Ordination is the seal which links the religious
community with the secular; or, if you like,
combines the two into a deeper unity. This too
is the goal of the university: all that rises must
converge, et cetera.

The cost of order is quite high; we do not yet
know what exactly the cost will come to. I am
one of the tiniest items below the line, some
rhombus stuck into the dike. What will it mean
for me to bear the cost of ordination? Both
my transition into this investiture—if they will
still have me, after this—and the higher orders
which bear upon us scoundrels fed on so many
books.

They have put me in a smaller cell temporarily;

this one has only artificial light. In confinement one seeks communion within; to see what it is we can see when we're really looking. I wish I could say what I had learned. Some of the revelations I considered great insights at the time I have since concluded false; while other things have remained nameless in my mind no matter how often I have tried to name them.

Which isn't, actually, all that often. Have you ever considered: which are things which should remain unnamed? These costs of order, rising, fill my cell with their dark light, and I close my eyes to be at peace in some world I do not understand.

"Dinner," they say at the door, but I don't move.

31.

I have to tell you now (I should have told you at the beginning): I do not find out the reasons for things. I had hoped, for a time, that that might be the reason for this narrative, but it is not.

Some men may find reasons easy; I am not one of them. But even if I did find them easy I can't make this story into the kind that solves the mystery.

I'm sorry. I know we want them all solved. With a little after finish on the tongue. This isn't this one. I had hoped it might be; but hopes are so often useless things.

Instead I will attempt to keep the story to the simplest of things: what happened.

I have no explanations. Not for Braunschweig, or even for myself.

32.

"What do you think theater is?" Hieram asks me.

"A show. A big show."

"What is it for?"

"People need it. The big show. To know who they are."

"And who are we, Thomas?"

"I don't know."

"I can see we haven't been doing our job. Watch again."

On the stage the man raises his head above the white bench in the black room, his monkey ears furry and huge. He tilts his head delicately from side to side, listening. His features are frozen and tense.

The music begins again, a 1980s synthesizer

motif, both annoying and affecting, sinking us into the pitch.

The man with the monkey ears tilts his head even farther, stretching his neck to its limit, looking for danger.

Like a medieval passion play, the figure of the sun emerges from stage right, Teletubbies cum Greek myth, a man in radiant yellow, with a huge starbust sun-head. A human sunflower, with a glowing smile and sympathetic eyes.

A smile spreads across the man with the monkey ears' face. He leans in to the sun.

Beside him, his wife's monkey ears are just seen to appear, poking over the edge of the bench.

The sun slowly moves across the stage. Both husband and wife monkey seem calmer, and they rise slowly onto the bench, where they settle in on their haunches.

The music introduces a flute for the critter emerging from stage left, rat, the actor crouched down in his dirty brown suit, looking with enormous eyes over the span of the black stage, he takes a step, then another.

With sudden violence in the music, the monkey people leap onto the rat and tear it open, spreading the red raffia paper streamers out of his belly, and feasting their mouths on the red juice, spreading it over their faces like clown paint. They make noises like birds, cooing gently to one another in pleasure. The rat's death sounds are quiet, barely heard.

The sun has left the stage and the moon rises back stage, her white face aglow in the lights. The monkey couple sit calmly, watching the lights move across the stage, placid Kabuki figures, Greek chorus sans lines, observing the motions of the heavens some distance from their bodies.

A timpani plays slow and rhythmic, and the lights fade to black.

Then they rise again.

The monkey man is wearing a suit. He lies still on a raised bed, a black figure on white sheets, his monkey ears catching the light. Only the sound of a clock ticking.

Now a woman's voice begins to sing, live, from just back stage. We do not see her. It is in a made up language; not one of any human community. But it feels as though we could understand it. Perhaps understanding it is unnecessary: the sounds themselves are the meaning.

The monkey man rises from the bed, his face full of terror, and hope. He clutches the sheet and stares off-stage after the woman's voice.

Her singing rises. We hear the sound of water.

She enters slowly, in silver glittering robes. Her voice rises to a crescendo, and the monkey man cowers in the bed. She approaches it, and when she reaches the edge of it, draws from her dress a long thin dagger.

At the climax of her singing, she gasps, and brings the dagger down onto the monkey man's chest.

Black out again. The sound of water remains.

We hear the stage crew rearranging furniture in the darkness. When the lights return, we are in a modern café, well-lit and pleasing, and the silver woman is now wearing professional urban attire, business skirt and blouse, sipping from her coffee. At a table near to her, the monkey man, still with his ears, types onto his laptop computer.

The rat enters, doing a hula dance, shaking his furry hips; the barista opens her mouth. The lights turn red, and the tables begin to shake. A fire alarm goes off, and the rat dances more and more wildly. Now we are bathed in the red light.

He climbs atop a table, which the monkey man and angel woman hold steady for him, and he raises his arms out towards the audience.

Black out. Again the sound of water.

At lights up we are in an office, with film posters on the wall. The monkey man, silver woman, rat and monkey woman are dressed in black, staring at their scripts.

They speak; we cannot hear their words. They're working. Arguing about something.

The monkey woman goes to look out the window. On the other side we see a child peering in. We watch them watch each other. The child raises its hand to tap against the glass. When he does, work stops. They all turn to stare at the window. The monkey woman turns to look at her workmates.

Suddenly everyone is even more excited about the script, and the monkey woman returns to her table and they all begin to work feverishly, making notes in pencil and passing them back and forth.

Music begins to play: 1960s Italian pop.

Hieram leans over to whisper in my ear: "You're the boy, you see? Looking in on what you can't understand. On what you can't have."

"That's not how I saw it at all," I say. "I saw you as the boy. Trapped in this hideous creation of your own making. A young Frankenstein."

The monkey woman looks up from her script very deliberately at me in the audience.

"Shhhh!"

We are both silent.

The boy begins to tap on the window again, and slowly, in a distracted manner, the monkey woman goes to the window and opens it, and the boy climbs through. She returns to her work as though nothing has happened. The child races around the office delightedly, staring at all the movie posters, and leaning over the shoulders of the adults at work. Finally he opens the office refrigerator, and when he sees all the food inside he smiles in delight.

Then the monkey man and woman, the angel woman, and the rat all rise, and shove the child into the refrigerator, pressing it closed and tight, over the sounds of the boy's screams.

Black out.

After a pause, the curtain rises on intermission.

"I need some wine," Hieram says. "Do you need anything?"

"I need to use the restroom."

"Wait until after the play."

I am still strapped in to my chair.

33.

The monkey lady is sprawled like an odalisque across a rectangular cube on stage; an abstract tableau. Yet I don't think the "curtain" has risen again; perhaps they're having technical difficulties. She's watching me, and I her.

The blue light is mystical; and her dark lipstick. Slowly the drums begin, and I see I have been fooled. The show has been continuing after all. They're war drums, slow and deliberate. When they pause the woman stands and opens her mouth:

"No more radiant sun was mine than Braunschweig, after the change. We'd eat peanut butter sandwiches in the bunker, and play poker for makeup and cookies. I knew I was chosen for something special; they told me in the briefing. And I was in love. I thought I could make it happen; make it go back to the person I had been before; it's silly to think so. What have you been thinking? Have you been to our town? What is it I should show you? My body? My dress? What do you think you have done here? Now that the dust has settled and winter has arrived, and we're proper again? Proper as raincoats and porridge. May Day and country hats. My father is dead. I'll never visit his grave again. In Slovenia they say the only good father is a dead one. Is he good now, as I am? Who will dig my grave when I have spoken my last? I'll take you with me; I promise; it isn't so far. Not so far. Just a little ways underground, past the station and the checkpoint, through the opium den, and down into the basement where I was made. I was made a woman. I was made into Braunschweig, to know nothing else."

Bum bum bum bum and I sit upright in my chair. Hieram leans over from behind my chair; I hadn't noticed he was there.

"She's good, isn't she?" he whispers. I don't reply. He leans closer in. "Would you like to know her? Biblically?" He cackles somehow as a whisper; it sounds like a dying wheeze.

34.

For some months after I was released, I was subject to ongoing waking nightmares. The kind that happen when you are asleep are bad enough, but the waking kind are rather more unpleasant. Voices in the head; visions in the sky. Sometimes it seemed summer had come; I had to make sure I still had my scarf and coat on so I would not freeze.

The dissertation was almost complete; now I barely remembered writing it. My advisor, however, was happy:

"It's great stuff, Thomas. Next month we'll have you as the featured reader at the Eschatology Conference; pick your favorite chapter and you're it!"

Henry was the only one who acted as though things were not right. He had always been a happy dog but now he rarely moved from his spot on the floor by my desk. His eyes searched mine for some explanation, but I had none.

On my refrigerator there was a note:

Gone south. Reach me on 28 Mhz on the shortwave.
— Bruno

I sat down next to Henry and ran my hand through his fur.

"I'm sorry, old buddy. I'm back now. I'm back."

35.

After intermission the torture began in earnest;
nor am I certain that it has yet ended. The turns
from which torture takes its name are mirrored
in so many life life-giving activities . . . they say
writers too are torturers. Bent into the turning
of the wheel.

I cannot say; I do not have an opinion; must
not. Only record, Thomas. Tell us what you
saw.

They brought a large knife before my face but
did not use it. Instead a man climbed underneath my chair and as they mimicked carving
me up with the blade, shoving it in and close,
past my body, so the man beneath me mimed
my screams for me; screams which soon became my own.

Only amateurs have to cut you open; the pro-
fessionals are already inside.

As the pacing of their stabbing and his screams
increased they wheeled out a magnificent 1930s

style curtain, veering wildly from its brass stands, leering crookedly across the open stage, a curtain for a proscenium which did not exist. Then the stage crew with great fanfare and joyous shouts, a real circus, tore the red gash aside and the pyramid stood there, gleaming white, and the woman began to sing again, impossibly high, like Mozart's Anna Storace, pouring out over the small theater, a kind of light to match the glowing pyramid.

Under her arcing voice the characters, rat, monkeys and angel don Commedia dell'Arte outfits and beat their drums, strapped across their chests, out from the pyramid, over to my chair, pounding until I am the center of a small and furious chain reaction, water and ice and light, searing me out of my mind—

36.

Chapters are like doors, or curtains: so easy to pretend that things stay on the other side of them.

I have been given an assignment to catalogue the chairs of the department over the course of its history, a task not made any easier by the room where the relevant biographical data are stored.

It's said that, as the city grows skyward, it also grows beneath, and this may be one of the rooms established in such digging, hastily layered in stone and then abandoned. It serves well as storage but Mr. Genevieve insisted the documents could not leave the room so I must study them here.

I had thought the lineage of the chairmanships should have been straightforward, but several of the earlier characters have complex histories; there is some question whether they are to be regarded as having actually worked for English.

I stare at a photo of one of them, an unassuming man, Taylor Codridtch, who is recorded as having served as chair for twenty years, but took an unspecified number of years off for alchemical research. Another, Janice Alketch, appears to have been an imposter. Not that she didn't get the degrees, but that she was not actually chairing English.

This would be an easy discrepancy to settle, I thought, but the problem quickly became embroiled in Byzantine power arrangements between the university's expanding bureaucracy in its early period of growth after the disaster, and I concluded the uncertainty surrounding her tenure stems chiefly from the department's ongoing discomfort with its own growing power.

We began as theology; I don't see how we could get more powerful than that. But my opinion is not the peer-reviewed source material sought for here.

I leave the papers and watch the simulated can-dles on the wall flicker. Henry hasn't been eating. He's happy when I take him to the dog park, but otherwise he sits by my bed unmoving, letting out dramatic sighs and farts. I'd take him to the vet but I can't afford it this month; my tenure "below decks," in the hands of the inquisition, is being taken out of my paycheck.

37.

That I have become a priest is not something that sits entirely well with me. Yet clearly I share with the long lineage of my predecessors a common longing for job security; what better source than religion? Yet we do not call it that. The illusion of church and state persists, though I cannot say how. Everyone knows who runs this town.

I checked in on the frequency Wenclas gave me; there was nothing but static. I even said "hello," into the band, but there was nothing. I fear he may have died in the cold; can he find heat in the country? I suppose some charitable farmer's wife may have taken him in. Or perhaps he did not leave at all; perhaps he is still here in the city, sending secret messages to all who will listen to him. That sounds like something he would do.

I saw Angela at the department party; she is said to have been engaged. But the look in her eye I do not like: it is the look of some of the initiates in the inquisition.

The word priest comes from *presbyter*—elder. We're supposed to be the ones who know what's going on. Yet I do not. Perhaps the word is a lie.

I have found so often that the process of writing down my experiences changes them; for good and bad. Perhaps because I tend to the pessimistic, at least regarding the effectiveness of whatever fights I've had with the world, I see the bad more easily:

1) In writing, it often seems to me the writing controls what happens in the story, and not the reverse. Perhaps this means I am not a good writer; this may well be the case. But wiser men than me have observed how language, being a slippery thing, so often finds ways to assert things we did not intend, or guides us along paths we had no desire to follow.

2) Writing always seems to become personal for me. I wish this were an authoritative narrative of the rise, decline and fall of Braunschweig. What a noble thing that might be! But

such things are beyond my power. Even when I desire that aspects of my narrative attain some worldliness—some real reality—beyond my own experience of them, inevitably the nature of that tale becomes even more personal.

3) I don't really know what I'm doing. What is authority, when I can claim none of it? So much of my life I have been a mere follower; even now I am one. It must be then, that I am not an author, even as I am not really a priest. Oh well.

It seems to me the act of writing—my work in trying to tell you what happened to me and my friends in my city—must be in part about working towards freedom. This ineffable thing, a thing I have become more and more certain is not about individuality at all, but about to-getherness, this thing seems to grow further and further away from me the more I write, as it is work I must do alone.

I don't mean to sound as though I am com-plaining. I remember that this is a great privi-lege. Even if I do it incompetently, and render no coherent or memorable story, it is work I am honored to do, even to fail at. It is just I am trying to understand what it is I am doing. I am sorry if that bothers you; it shouldn't. It means that I am taking you seriously. I hope, very much, that you will understand more than me.

The work is taking me away from Braunschweig; it is taking me closer to you, and to me. I don't know what that might mean. Perhaps it doesn't need to mean anything, even if it is true.

I have to leave Braunschweig; but I don't know how.

38.

I have been following Angela to see where she goes. My superiors made it clear to me that I would regret it if I revealed the happenings beneath our city . . . our theatrical productions. They also suggested I would be punished if I tried to leave. They didn't say anything about what would happen if instead I tried to get deeper inside.

She pauses outside the door and whispers into the grating beside it. She's wearing red, like a cardinal. Or concubine. Yet I suspect the thing she is bound to is not human.

I step up to the grate after she has passed through the door.

"Let me in," I whisper.

"Thomas, what are you doing here?" The voice is familiar, but I can't place it.

"Mr. Genevieve wanted me to deliver a message."

I hear the click on the door and step into the vestibule.

Will I desire her more or less once I know what she is doing? Once I see that she has joined with the body of secret worshippers? Although it disgusts me I find myself drawn to the power of it; how many have felt the same? Drawn in despite their better judgment?

I go down the stairs; the fluorescents are flickering. They go down a long way.

At the end of them, another hall, lit now by torchlight. Beyond that, one of their sanctums. The slave hands me the leads and I attach them to the back of my head; I have the feeling I've done this before. Angela smiles from across the room; she is strapped in to the wall, her eyes covered with glasses, and her skull also covered with leads.

"Let me help you, sir," the slave says, and I do as he asks, stepping in to the restraints and leaning back into them, against the wall. He places the leads against the back of my head.

He hands me silvery ear phones, which I put into my ears.

"Do you wish glasses?"

"No, I am meditating."

One of the functions of the machine is simple guided meditation; as you move closer towards an alpha state, bird song plays in the distance, to move you closer in. If you grow distracted, rain begins, and then thunder, to guide you gently back towards the hidden center.

39.

Pierre Paul Broca. My nemesis. Not much makes sense any more. Are there people for whom these things make sense?

The city is shadowed over my room; my books are watching me from the shelf. Broca's area is not exclusive to language, the latest neuroscientists tell us, but still central. Perhaps my notion of the conspiracies running my city are still entirely naïve—perhaps they have been in control of my narrative the entire time! Amusing. The problem with conspiracy is when it is used to absolve you of your own faults. I will have to work harder to avoid that.

The experience of the cabal's hidden communion there in the basement is not unlike graduate study—minus the discussion. The brain is tricked into arriving at the feeling of mutual understanding—but I do not know what it is we understood.

Now I am cowering in my bed. Henry is lying on the floor. The night of Braunschweig seems an infinite haven; but I don't know which door to open.

The radio is crackling on my desk.

"Thomas . . . are you there?"

I wrap my blankets around me in the cold and step to my desk. Henry is smiling at my feet.

I press the transmit button.

"Yes? Wenclas?"

"I need you to come to the border. Can you come?"

"Yes."

40.

Our ancestors explained extranormal psychological states using gods: the more extreme the state, the greater the god. Archaeologists, on the other hand, point out that dramatic structures encode those states themselves. In the presence of gigantic columns and strange stone faces, the human being can't help but feel some echo of the crafters' deliberate intentions.

It's too easy to surmise, like Freud, that the human mind has "unplumbable depths" and "irrational logics" that lead nowhere.

I know these states are directional. The same as our ancestors knew. They are pushing me in a particular direction.

I'm packing my backpack. Putting on my earmuffs. The snow is coming down; and the light from the sun is refracted through the white sky in ripples, like the ocean.

41.

Inside my mind is this vista of color, contrapuntal to the colorlessness of our modern
dress: some art project I will never be able to
achieve as I am not one of the great conceptual
artists of the late 20th Century . . . Kandinsky
/ Pollock splatters in huge globules all around
the gallery and the city surrounding it, on the
sidewalk and the alleyways, over the street. An
explosion of color.

I can feel the splatters around me as Henry
and I step out of the apartment building; little
nubbins of electric imagination. I rub Henry's
head and step into the snow.

42.

It has begun to rain. I can't see a thing. The water turns to ice when it hits the earth, turning the path into an ice rink. Henry and I take shelter under an oak, watching the storm. My radio is dead; or rather, it transmits only static.

The sound of the rain is so soothing, even though it could surely kill me. I set about looking for the ingredients for a fire.

I tie a tarp into the branches above, after much cursing and scuffling. Enough shelter for a tiny flame. Henry watches me blow on the kindling patiently. He's listening for wolves, perhaps, or for some memory he has of the landscape.

I know now why I came to Braunschweig. The weight of it, teetering massive over the sky, but more importantly in the mind, has on me the opposite effect, of weightlessness: I have yet to stop floating.

I wonder who the Brown was who gave us Brown Clan, Braunschweig. Was he a good or a cruel chieftain? Or both? He must have had a good dog like Henry.

43.

City comes from the proto indo-european *kei*;
to lie: lie down with me in the city, included
in its secondary ancient sense "beloved, dear,"
dearer to me than anything, in our place upon
a mountain, or beneath it, rising with the sea,
and the earth, over our fate.

44.

Who can say what these phantoms mean, swarming over me in waves, the armaments of war for men long dead, or yet to be—still to be—I will not, though I crave it, succumb to its grave melodies of hope; not yet; for I still have my weight to carry home. Who should abide by such grave messages but the outcast; never plumbing his course until after he's sunk into the deep?

'Tis a mute must rock, lashing his time out, with a strung sorry load of fortunes: still marching into the rock iron fortress of this night; not mine; not yet mine; I will not; not yet, be so sallow as to meet its vicious entrances with any greeting, nor any bow; not yet; it will not be my words who enter into its hypnotisms and traceries unforgiving; for I can bear any archer's stare, or any mile, even this one: I promise.

45.

Wenclas's beard is wet, dripping into the snow. Over the fire he looks like a German warrior from the Dark Ages. Henry goes and licks his hand.

"The radio's not working," Wenclas says.

The white landscape feels somehow non-threatening, though I know it is very dangerous. I stand by the fire and warm my hands.

"Shall we get some firewood?" I say.

"How did you find me?"

"I saw the smoke."

Behind him is an ancient stone hut.

"Is it a camping lodge?"

"Yes."

"Do you want some potato chips?"

I hand him the bag. The crumbs stick to his beard, along with the snow.

"How long are we going to be here?" I ask.

"I don't know. Probably not long. The signal is in and out."

The radio buzzes and crackles then, at his feet. And then hums.

"There," he says, like for a lover.

46.

We're moving over the landscape, men now reciting the names of the work, work not set in the hour, but the moment; before there were minutes, there were moments.

That is the work of walking in the snow, listening to the crunch, and the silence, and the occasional hum of the radio, like the burr of a crow on the black grass waving up over the hills washed in white.

The act of walking is itself a relief; it needn't rely on anything else. There are no expectations other than the walking's beginning and end, which are thankfully distant.

To me it takes on a religious character, and it does not surprise me that pilgrimages of various religions should take walking as its central character; perhaps the religions are walking itself, more than the saint or holy shrine that is intended. Chaucer knew as much, surely, since we never get to the shrine with him.

There is too a terrible gravity to walking; Beckett knew that; I am tempted to emulate him and expand this chapter of the narrative into a large and emptying field of some strange spirit, but knowing that I am not as wise as he, I would fear the great wide space doing so would summon, and will content myself with a moment or two spent in its shadow.

In the blending of the white sky with the white plain, I feel as sailors must at sea, only shades of color to distinguish between them. The path is only a slight depression in the field. The radio is warm and squawks like a bird.

I who have been, as it were, the prisoner of religion, find I appreciate its character more and more the further it travels from the source (or closer to it, depending on your perspective). Perhaps this is how so many medieval clerics justified their labors, knowing the works of men to be the imperfect shadows of divine ends, they could forgive their institutions' thousand failures if only once or twice it managed to capture the peculiar majesty of nature.

Wenclas is a good walker and does not tire; I drink without stopping from my canteen so as not to delay him.

47.

Henry, I know, could walk farther than us both.
He stops suddenly on the top of the slow rise,
no more than a dozen meters or so above the
flood plain, and whines.

The radio then begins to speak.

"Here, one, nine, seventy-seven. Here is one,
nine, seventy-seven, here—"

It cuts off. Henry has begun to growl, low in
his throat.

We all stop and listen.

The silence is the most beautiful sound.

48.

The crow watches us approach the stone barrow, sitting atop it, lookout. The gray stones
poke out of the snow, its distinctive shape
clearly one of the burial mounds known in this
region. He lifts one foot, then the other, exam-
ining his body, then setting his eyes back on
us. Then he turns into the air and alights, his
wings spreading into the falling snow, a curved
black razor.

Over the sky he turns, listening to the sounds
of the earth; our footsteps, and a train in the
far distance, too far for us to see, we can just
barely hear its vibrations. He listens for the
sound of his mate back from hunting, circling
the air like a hawk, watching the sky from yellow down to blue, and white. Waiting to come
home.

"That's where the signal is coming from,"
Wenclas says, and I stoop down to the barrow
entrance, to peer into the chamber. I can still
feel the crow above, like my twin.

The inhabitants of the region returned to their ancient rites in the aftermath of the nuclear event, and buried their many dead in the tumuli used by Neolithic Man, because they could be seen over a great distance, so your brethren would always feel close, from the window, even when you could not venture outside.

"I don't see a transmitter," I say.

"Can you fit through the opening?"

"I think."

He hands me his lighter, and I press my palms against the frozen earth and scoot my body through the gap between the gateway stone and the dirt, wriggling like a fish. Inside I flick the lighter and am greeted by the skull of a child, no larger than my fist, shrunken as though by heat.

Around it the bones are arranged in decoration, lines meeting lines, humeri to ulnus to fibula. The picture of the body, greeting the worlds to come.

"What do you see?"

"Bones!"

"What else?"

Sitting atop the skull is a metal block, tinged with blue.

"Here."

I toss it outside the barrow; graverobbing.

49.

The little beast is a second radio, pulsing us towards a more distant signal: breadcrumbs for we children. It hums when aligned; we take turns holding it before us like a divining rod.

The ordination I have been seeking in Braunschweig is mirrored in the ordination of the countryside: these deeper orders provide nourishment for we little seekers, the scribes and missives tumbling through space. I can see them as trembling white lines underneath the air. Ley lines; marks of the plane.

I imagine so many of our ancestors must have been following signals; from before we even came to this earth. The tiniest particles, listening to sound.

As spiders sense the electrical fields of the earth to balloon into the air and soar, so we lift our heads into the bitter wind to follow our warm hum.

The world seems deadened but for the signal;

my gnawing hunger pang is gone. Wenclas too I see is somewhat sedated by our new friend. We hear the Lady of the Lake and walk in her rhythm, unable to stomach anything but the thought of Her.

50.

Angela has been calling. I can hear her as a distant voice in my head. Like a distant fairy, calling from Fairyland.

"Not now," I whisper. "Not now."

Her voice is like a fly, veering into nearby orbits. Overhead the aurora borealis have begun, shimmering green curtains billowing in the breeze.

"I need you to listen," she whispers.

"Shhhh, shhhh."

"You're in danger," she says.

"You're a bitch."

"Yes, but you're still in danger."

"Shh, shhh."

51.

The colors, which are waves, I'm underneath them, I am; not just a man. who will tell me how it is—who it is—which it is; tell me: what do the colors mean?

I know now that light is alive—its behavior no more predictable than Man—but the origin of light is just as obscure as the origin of cellular matter.

Likely it is trying communicate with us, and that is the maelstrom I see, Wenclas too, stumbling under the weight of the collisions in the air.

Perhaps life itself is the emergent property of transition states, as from photon to wave, and boy to man.

One of my friends at university, in studying Klein-Gordon relativity fields, once told me that the various states of matter are friends in conversation, but through impenetrable walls. Somehow life crosses them, as we cross this wasteland.

"I can't see my feet," Wenclas says.

I nod, smiling. The colors are growing stronger.

Suddenly it occurs to me that much of my work is in opposition to the 20th century physicist Richard Feynman, who wanted to assign humanities to the dustbin of history.

The consequences of his prejudice, and men like him, have had consequences Braunschweig is still dealing with.

Sometimes I even suspect it was Feynman led to the war.

The rainbow is alive, and I and Wenclas in it, no trouble any more, mama, I've left it all behind.

Part 3

52.

Order, from the Italic *ord, "to arrange, weave" in turn from the Proto-Indo-European *ar: "to fit together," also the source of "art" and "arm."

To ordinate then—to set in order and arrangement—and to be ordinated—set into the order by some greater power—is about armament, a kind of training, as any student of these medieval institutions can attest. Not only conquering but ruling. No warmonger succeeds without his priests in alliance, to follow behind and weave the stories which will order the booty, women, jewels, roads, dances and significances of our culture, stubborn mule in the mud.

To ordinate—and be ordinated—is to allow yourself to be set into the loom, while you too loom, and lumber however slow to recreate your pattern's movements in the smaller realm still within your power.

Arm me with words, father, and set me in arrangement, for I shall divine by my spirit whose hand is needed where in the assault on reality.

- -

Reality means bequeathement: dowry patrimony and legend, hat sword and gun, dog butter and map, grammar and hasp, hoe and yard.

But in its mutation—the greedy slippage in DNA and woof and weave—as Feynman observed in his famous 1979 lectures in New Zealand: the rules of nature are simple, it's just that everyone is playing them at once.

This is why Rome kept her armaments, until Caesar, outside the pomerium: having armed us, it is never clear precisely we will turn, agonize under X-ray, to assert this new authority over the woven field of bequeathement. Over all we see.

Having reached the edge then, of our secret pomerium, Wenclas and I discovered how far the world had come from the cloistered enclave we had known in Braunschweig.

It continues to amaze me how little intelligence people attribute to animals—as though we were not animals ourselves. In keeping with this, many people also see animals as monoliths: all dogs are the same, all cats, all birds, etc. And I don't just mean speciation—even the stubbornest anthropocentrist sees these obvious differences—but cultural differences. Italian cats are not the same as Finnish cats, even if they have the same coloration. German dogs are not the same as English dogs, even if they are both labrador retrievers. Anyone who has really studied animals and cultures will not be surprised by this.

So it was that Henry showed us the way out of the rainbow—he was the first to see the secret it contained. Of course, he is a sensitive dog, likely a better student of culture than me.

53.

I can hear the horse behind us. Wenclas turns his head to look. Henry dashes between my legs towards the sound of the hooves.

Human and dog evolution diverged 60 million years ago; we're closer to bats. Anthropologists tell us one reason dogs and humans hunted so well together is the whites of our eyes: white sclera allowed dogs to see where we were looking with some precision.

Etymologically, the word dog is untraceable. It disappears beyond time's event horizon, in our long millennia together. (*Perro* is similarly untraceable).

I could not say how Henry knew what was to come; I would have to be a dog. Often I have thought that animals, especially dogs, could sense spirits—perhaps they are even instrumental in the creation of them, through an act of the dog imagination.

Yes, dogs have imagination. How else would

we share so much with them, if there were not a space in the imagination to lay our dreams out and examine them, as a dog examines his sleeping place?

I turned and saw Henry chase the rider through the mist; I ran to follow, signaling to Wenclas.

I could hear Henry in the distance, but the sound was distorted in the close air. I ran.

"Henry!"

He barked back. The horse I could not hear at all. Behind me I could hear Wenclas.

Then I could see Henry, and the rider, who reached down from his horse towards the dog, who smelled his hand.

"Henry!"

Then they were both gone.

A patch in the mist cleared and I ran to where they'd been. The green moss looked bright against the white mist. I could see nothing past it.

I called his name again. In the distance I heard a faint bark, and ran for it.

I could hear the trees in the wind. They were telling me something. Some great thing. I wanted to speak their language but I couldn't. Not yet.

What is it? They're telling me where he's gone.

The moss is growing thicker, almost like snow. Sopping wet and dripping down below the roots into the grove.

I realize the copse is warm. It's generating heat somehow. The trees whistle overhead, telling me . . .

Wenclas stumbles into the glade.

"Where did they go?"

"I heard them but they've gone. I can't hear

them now. What is this place? It's warm."

Below my feet I heard a distant sound. Henry.

"He's below."

"Likely it's part of the same tunnel system," Wenclas said. "There must be an entrance here."

He began to peer over the roots of the trees, searching for it.

I saw a light through the trees, peering into the shadow where we stood. It stirred a powerful memory in me.

That isn't quite the right word, I know. Not a memory, but I don't know what it is. Something from my mind, perhaps, but also something else.

It reminded me of the walks I used to take in the summers, when it seemed the snow would melt, but did not, and the carefully heated hedgerows through the university gardens provided that illusion in spades: of some ancient glade, safe from harm.

Now we were in a real ancient glade. The sight of the green had stirred something in me, something that wanted to get out.

Wenclas was looking at me.

"What is it?"

"Nothing. Do you see anything?"

"Not right here. You saw something. What was it?"

"It doesn't matter. Just something I remembered. Come on, we should find him, before he gets lost."

The route through the university garden is a maze, bent at each entrance in towards the center, as is the tradition. Each leaf is distinct if you take the walk early in the afternoon, so that some light still penetrates the maze but is not directly overhead. Every surface gleams.

Around the world in many places, ancient human paths are marked by plants, who grow around them from long habit. The maze was like that, only more magical, because it seemed to invite the possibility that the world you left outside the maze was not real, and as you came closer in to its center, you were approaching the real world, heretofore hidden. Of course, this is also the thesis of Braunschweig. We terrible scholars hiding from the light and the world. From one another. Building our lies to combat the truth outside.

"Are you all right?"

"Yes. Did you find anything?"

"Here."

He thrust his boot through some branches, revealing a passageway below. It smelled of deep earth and loam, and Henry.

I crawled down inside, and Wenclas followed.

54.

The tunnel stretched into complete darkness, but I could hear something up ahead. Not Henry. But something.

"I brought this," Wenclas said, and strapped a huge light onto his forehead.

"You came prepared."

He smiled slightly and went around me, into the dark.

The light flashed huge shadows through the tunnel, and our sounds echoed up and back, mixing with the sound I heard ahead.

Some kind of animal.

I was back in the maze again, watching the light play over the gleaming green leaves. The seeker must wind his way around into the maze, and time slows down as he does, like thickening liquid, exposed to the air. As he approaches the center, each step seems to take a very long time.

I realized I would have to go into it. I could not stay eddying on its edges forever.

"Do you smell that?" Wenclas asked.

"Yes. Keep going."

A terrible musk.

We followed the tunnel into a curve, when Wenclas' boot caught in the dirt.

Flashing ahead in his light were the horns.

The minotaur.

I cried out, and then the thing spoke.

It was a man, I realized. A shaman, chanting, in his mask. Around him danced Henry, moving as I had never seen him. I felt I understood the language, but I did not know it. The man spun in the chamber, illuminated by his torches.

"Who are you!" shouted Wenclas.

The man replied but in the same language. we moved closer. Henry ran to me, his eyes wide and happy.

"Good dog. Good dog."

The man's dance intensified, and he attached to his bullhead various gleaming objects, silver fire in the yellow light.

"I know you!" the minotaur shouted, in English.

Suddenly I could feel the clouds overhead, the same way I had felt the crow. I was the crow, soaring in the light, bright over the day, a menace to my enemies.

I felt the urge to approach the shaman and kneel, however absurd. Instead I approached his sanctum, and watched him dance.

I closed my eyes and could see the red orbs of his torches glowing behind my eyelids. Nearby I could feel Wenclas, and to my right, Henry.

In silence we listened to his whispers, little mutterings on his lips. A great weight gathered in the air—a heavy, invisible cloud. We listened, together. The shaman had also stopped speaking.

The cloud seemed at once foreign and part of us; both threat and friend. I began to sing and the darkness moved around me, still with my eyes closed.

Now we were dancing together, just as we had with Mr. Genevieve in our ritual end-of-semester whirling dances, but now it was more serious. Now we were independent.

55.

I don't know—and perhaps I shouldn't say—
just what it is I intend with this narrative. I had
thought it was a warning, or last testament.
The kind of crazed Gnostic document secret-
ed away in the desert to insult some vanished
tribe; but no. I can't leave Braunschweig like I
had thought; leaving only draws you closer in:

- -

The university has as one of its central com-
ponents the thesis of empire—"making into
one"—similar to the motto of the late American republic. This can be beneficial, even as
cells are the result of a dozen animalcules fused
together into a being acting under a common
purpose. But no one can defend empire unre-
servedly. So much is lost. It may be I am one
of the lost things.

"Have you come far?" the shaman asked.

"From the city, " I said.

"Mm. Very bad there."

"Is it?"

"Yes. You will need to be purified, if you stay."

"What were you doing with Henry?"

"I communicate with animals. Just like I communicate with you. He told me a story."

"What did he tell you?"

"That it's time for you to go."

He stood from the fire where we had eaten. I felt dizzy; Wenclas was already outside.

"Follow your dog. He knows where he is going."

Henry is a royal name; to go with his peasant face.

I head back out into the light.

Who should shield me in the dark when I grow old; wraith of time, corded around my gut, turn me underneath the water. Let me see the face of the deep.

56.

"Likely we could follow the tunnels all the way back. We could if a storm comes. But I still want to find the signal," Wenclas said.

"Who made this thing?" I said, holding the blue metal I found in the grave.

"The people we have to find."

Over the rainbow, and through the woods, to grandmother's house we go:

- -

I don't know, or shouldn't say; can't say. I know Henry understands more than me. what is it you understand, you goddamned dog? I want you to explain it to me.

Henry understands as well as me and Wenclas that we have to go on. But he understands something else as well. Has some idea, perhaps, what it is we'll find.

"What did you tell that old man, hmm?"

Henry just smiles at me.

Perhaps the light is the answer. There's no more sign of the rainbows we passed through but it still seems I can feel them in the air, near enough to touch.

Almost I feel it is a cliché to assert the journey changed me; it is what journeys are for, after all. The question is the degree, the reason, and what I did with it. Really I do not know: increasingly I feel I have lost all bearings or any measuring system whereby I would be able to order the experiences I shared with Wenclas outside of Braunschweig.

Later I realized we had already entered a region from which it is possible there is no escape.

57.

Identity is in repetition: *idem et idem* is the root of the word, "again and again." So too for Wenclas and I after we met the shaman: we found ourselves retracing our steps. Not once or twice, but hundreds of times.

What follows is what Wenclas and I managed to reconstruct based on our conversations after we believed we had escaped:

58.

Orbit one:
The path begins to change

I heard a scraping sound, as of a huge stone being shifted into place; when I turned to look, Wenclas had vanished.

What whim is it in the world, who rakes the path in our garden? I stumble into its runnel in the earth, invisible but deeper because of it.

What is it in me who would escape, and what would it mean to escape?

Return to orbit. Exit this plane. Let me out, captain; I need no parachute. I have my life. Ready to roar; and create:

The trees are drifting closer, like birds, moving slow over the ground.

Lights in the sky; and in my head.

The trees are speaking too; what are they say-ing? Like the tree outside my building, cut into the night against the brick, leaning in, to whisper:

The scraping sound is the rake of the gardener in the garden, moving over the sand, shifting it into place, over my face:

The whisper of my own head is disorienting, like the trees: which part of myself am I in? Like Robert Ashley says: can the self change? What part of the body does the self reside in? The 20th Century is gone but it is still haunts my bones and nerves, legacy residue: archaeological strata stuck under my skin, to lift my consciousness up, and assert this strange authority:

The voice says,

"Now you're getting closer."

"Closer to what?" I say.

"Closer to the stars."

What is it turning underneath the drum of my skull, to lock me in to the thing below, somnambulant bend down to the drumming beneath, the forest floor and its magnets, shifting slowly west, turning my feet:

"What's happening?"

"You're being drugged," it says.

"Who's drugging me?"

"Who do you want it to be?"

In down and left, to span the target's whet and whistle for the drum, whose voice, so like my own, penetrates the soles of my feet, to keep me drumming down, down underneath the trees:

It may be the act of imagining a spiral is itself enough to generate its pull, knowing it exists there in your mind the gravity of each step is curved in towards its invisible center:

The target is not the forest. Nor is it the trees.

It's the journey itself, or this part of it, the bending force of my steps now, rumbling low, and lower, bereft:

The fear of the step makes its own music, because we can imagine what may be in store with each successive series of inches, cutting the time left in two, and two, and two . . .

"What is it you're afraid of?"

"You. I'm afraid of you."

But I'm always afraid now; perhaps that's what I'll grow to understand: fear, or its closest cousins, these inhabitants of the realm I lived in for so long without realizing what it was.

This thing, the realm of the spirits, which is not some other world but this one, the one that you all know, table, chair, refrigerator, tree, glass, dog, plate, hat, shoes and key-chain, the realm of the spirits, who inhabit us with an eye to evading not only logic but time. Which is not to say that they succeed in evading it, not completely. We build over them, weed into them, sew parts onto them, in the horror of our own recovery.

We think we have the story but of course we don't. We think there are reasons, and there are, but we've been provided with the wrong ones. We think we can see where we are going; we cannot; we believe there is order, and there is, but its depth so far outpaces the length of our legs, arms, head, and vision that most often we do not even begin to speak of it, let alone start, or understand the faintest bit of it.

You know it is a foreign country though, if you are honest. Hat, dog, chicken, dress, paint can, road, church, river, woman. You know it is something put upon you, a burden you aren't even able to see, in seeing it.

So I should say it has been this great gift to be imprisoned in this chamber of horrors, Wenclas and I. Though I had known for some time that we had enrolled in an ancient religious cult by seeking degrees at university I hadn't realized quite how far that cult extended. I had thought it quaint. Perhaps it even is quaint, in the way Leviathan might be quaint, or a black hole. Just some other feature of reality ready to swallow you whole.

The order of the orbit is one of slowing down. Just like the hippies of a former century would advise you: be present in the moment. Be mindful of the passing of time. But unlike those glamorous pre-lapsarian figures whose only desire was more pleasure, both physical and mental, the order of this orbit around the secret center of the nature of the forest is to slow down time with a mind to rend your skin from off of your face and get you to be properly analytical about the experience. Philosophy may well be a form of torture in any context but here it attains a purity I still have some trouble describing.

Really, that was all it was. I found myself back with Wenclas soon enough; though at the same time, as has so often been the case with the things I experienced after leaving my old world behind, I never really stopped being there on the slow spiral into the dark wood, step by step by step.

I told Wenclas what had happened and we stopped to talk.

"What is it," he said.

"Some kind of door without a key. I don't know. It's crazy. Absolutely insane. But it was real."

"Tell me what you think it means."

"I think it means we're getting closer. Closer to whatever this thing is. Closer to whatever it might mean to us."

"What is it?"

"I don't know," I said. "Pain, maybe. Angst. Fear. Some kind of tempest of the mind, held under water, drowning. But still alive. Drowning eternally, and trying to take us with it."

"Yes, I feel that too," he said. "Like a depressed person who wants to take you with them. A suicide looking to make it a double suicide."

"But it has a light to it too; inside of the torture there's an awareness of what it means, the slowness itself, it's somehow important. The process of the meditation."

"It is very dangerous. Perhaps any kind of meditation! It's going to happen again, I know. The shaman must have poisoned us. Do you think?"

"No, I don't think that's what it is. It's something more fundamental than that. Something like what the poison might cover up. The journey itself. Thank you for talking, Wenclas. I thought you would think I was mad."

"But you are mad. That's why I brought you."

59.

Orbit two:

Wenclas

The snow fell in globs, melting down Wenclas' back, and turning the world white. Overhead he could still see patches of the sky; purple edging into black, stuck with stars.

He tried to find the trees to seek shelter, but they'd turned invisible behind the white.

White, wet, winter—all versions of the same word—seemed focused on reducing Wenclas to his constituent atoms.

He called out to Thomas, and then Henry, but heard nothing. He walked in a straight line, measuring the distance of his boots from one another, to take his mind off disaster. He raised his head to the sky; a satellite coursed over the bald patch. He felt the sky shift closer; like the lens of a microscope.

The jittery feeling inside of him increased; the satellite seemed to grow closer, shooting in a descending orbit. A small white light fanned into one larger.

The snow felt like quicksand, sucking him down. The satellite was too bright; it painted the snow with its light, grim but somehow inviting. The arc of the stars moving over him filled him with dread. He could not remember which direction he'd been moving in.

He looked up again; the satellite had passed over the horizon, but its path remained visible, like a meteor in slow motion. He had the overwhelming feeling of déjà vu, but not one hinting at a distant past come again but rather a time much closer by. The minutes he'd spent searching for Thomas in the snow—had it been minutes?—now seemed to have come again. He would have to dig a shelter or he would freeze.

But as soon as the thought came to him the air became translucent again; he saw a figure ahead and he cried out. Thomas—was it him?—turned, at the sound of his voice.

Now the snow was less a problem than the feeling that was growing inside of him—some aberration had occurred. He needed to sleep—he knew that—but he wasn't sure sleep would heal this particular malady. Once again the satellite peered over the edge of the far horizon; climbing, climbing. Satellites couldn't orbit that fast, could they?

A conviction grew inside him mind that this was deliberate: some Cartesian evil demon had harnessed him in its faraway lair, and had set about obscure Chinese tortures to drive him mad.

The snow slipped again behind his back, and once again the satellite rose on the horizon and he closed his eyes, willing this hallucination to pass. In the darkness behind his eyelids time seemed to slow down even more. The space between drawing a breath in and letting it out became a very long time indeed.

60.

Orbit three

I don't really know how to describe it, nor do I know if it is important for this narrative. I have no idea what is and is not important here, from beginning to end. My hope is that the task of setting it down into words will reveal something to me about how to interpret my experiences.

At the time I was completely convinced, in a queer inner logic that approximates that of dreams, that I had been sucked into a kabbalistic nightmare, one central to the temples of the ancient Near East, wherein a supplicant, or victim, or both, was confined in the temple and forced to move along a wall in near darkness.

With each successive inch the supplicant advanced, time would slow down at a proportionate rate. Just as, from the perspective of the observer, the astronaut falling into the black hole appears asymptotically closer but never enters, so the tortured supplicant to Kabala approaches the heart of the temple, and ensures his own madness and damnation in doing so.

I am reminded of Xeno's paradox of the tortoise and the hare. Curiously, history records a young college student solving the ancient paradox sometime in the early 21st Century, though not all were convinced. His argument was that, time being fluid, it must move forward. It is impossible to cut time into infinitely smaller increments. Perhaps I agree with that young student, yet I fear he was not acquainted with the psychological torture mechanisms I encountered in the trapped spaces of the Braunschweig wilderness. Perhaps that doesn't matter either: the increments were small enough to drive me mad.

Yet too I find I am grateful to all of this—all of this horror. Allow me to relish one of these rare moments of gratitude. They brought me here, to my house, in the wilderness. I have not mentioned it before. It is just a house. Looking over the trees. The village has little to do with me, or I with it. But it was the torture—I am convinced of this—that allowed me to come here.

61.

Orbit Four:

Wenclas

The storm had passed; Wenclas emerged from the white blindness of the storm and saw me sitting on a stump, staring at my hand.

"Are you all right?" he said.

"No," I said. "No I'm not."

"What happened?"

"You tell me first," I said.

"I don't know. I don't feel well either. Where is Henry?"

"I haven't seen him. But I don't think he's far. What do you think is happening?"

"We must be close to the center of the signal. It's distorting our reason. It's a weapon.

Something that was used in the war, and never turned off. Maybe they couldn't turn it off."

"What is it?"

"It probably stimulates the hippocampus. But there's other aspects too. They may have perfected the technique of broadcasting encoded visual stimuli: television signals, but the receiver is our brains."

"That sounds unpleasant."

"Of course, I could be wrong. I don't actually know much more than you. Can you stand up?"

"Yes."

"Let's find Henry. And keep talking; it's easier if we do."

62.

Disjunct

So much of this has been a lie. It's better I stop now, than that I continue, but I know that I will not.

What do you want to believe about my city? I wish I could ask you. What do you believe about your own? What do you believe happens when so many people get together in a space? And what do you believe happens to you specifically, in that space?

Are you still recording, Thomas?

Yes

Why?

To try and answer that question.

You'll have to stop soon.

- -

I know that I am in some danger of repeating myself. Perhaps that does not matter any more. The number of people who read this document is destined to be very few; and it will be entirely in their power to destroy it. Perhaps this will serve as a form of amusement to them, just as generations of captives may on occasion have their prize daughter elected to a position of some status by her generational owners, who find it titillating to have her recite the ancestral war-cries and denounce her overlords.

Well. The problem with leaving is that it is temporary. The only true leavetaking is death; and for some, even that does not serve as sufficient exit. As with so many things, it revolves around the question of desire: what is it, Thomas, O Deep One, that you want?

Do I want Angela? And at what price?

I look at my surroundings now: these bourgeois trappings, the comfortable result of compromise. Edward Gibbon scribbling away in the countryside, safe from the front lines of the teeth of his "betters" . . .

Better, better, best . . .

I know now better what kinds of weapons exist out here in the wilderness. Wenclas wanted that we should harness one of them, but I could not. I betrayed him, if you like. Or did not follow him in deep enough.

What is it that I expect to find?

We're going to have to begin at the beginning again . . .

O how I hate to do this.

Don't you already know this story?

Wasn't it taught to you as a child?

No, you have forgotten.

Here we go again:

63.

Why is it easier to imagine holocausts overseas? Easier to think of history as distant? Easier to imagine atrocities occur only behind enemy lines, in some other town, village, nation, family?

When did we become so accustomed to Dr. Pangloss's sweet drinks, reading Genesis and imagining ourselves the king of all creation, moving towards the best of all possible worlds?

Maybe there is no point in time to identify; only a habit of mind.

To see the holocaust nearby one has to admit one can commit one. To see history in your kitchen one has to know you are the ignorant medieval peasant future children will laugh about in class.

It becomes even more difficult when we speak of government, structures of power, bosses.

In the past, kings practiced human sacrifice.

History records this. So do the Bible and other stories. Easy to imagine the times distant and safe. To believe that science has freed us from superstition; that the Enlightenment has banished despots with flesh stuck on their teeth.

To quote the film from the early 21st century:

"What if I told you . . ."

What if I told you.

What if I told.

Tattle-tale.

Teller of tales.

All storytellers are guilty. All have betrayed.

We open our mouth to speak:

64.

I was never granted any extraordinary privileges. Perhaps that is why I am writing this narrative. Otherwise I would have taken it all as a matter of course. Bred to the purpose; as some of them are.

It may also be that I am not the person to write this story; everything which I thought would be bearable has become more and more difficult the closer I get to telling it.

The electronics attached to my head in the basement, and the little prison theatricals I described were bucolic interludes compared with what came later. After I returned. After Wenclas and I failed.

Also it becomes clearer to me that trauma is not best suited to prose; I should have stuck to verse. Or theater. Or drugs. Yet part of me remains committed to the factual relation of the events I know transpired, and prose is the demon for that. Demon is definitely the right word.

What is a demon? Only a thing inside you. Like a genetic switch, waiting to be turned on:

65.

Wenclas, Henry and I sat in the cave watching the light slip from the horizon. We had poured water over the roof to seal the snow into ice, and made "beds" from carved snow, so the cold air would pool below where our bodies lay.

"It was a timelessness then, that you experienced," I said.

"Yes, a very slow time."

"What do you think its purpose is?"

"Other than as an instrument of torture? I'm not sure. What did you see?"

"There was a satellite overhead. It seemed to grow closer as I watched."

"What do you think it means?"

"I don't know. It was very frightening. Even more so than the time dilation; at least with that I had the feeling that it would end. The satellite was something foreign. A threat. Or it could have been; I don't know. How much of these experiences are hallucination?"

"Not as much as you may think. Do you think it was a ship?"

"I don't know. It could have been. A ship would look like a satellite, wouldn't it? If it were in orbit."

"Did you see anything else?"

"I want to know what we're going to do when we find the signal's origin."

"It depends on what it is. I don't think it's some lone beacon. I think we'll find the people using it."

"And what then?"

"I don't know."

Outside I saw the crow again, lingering over

the receding shadow of the sun. I wanted to be with him, watching from the air as the earth slipped into night.

66.

We kept walking. The time dilation had not abated but we were not separated and it was easier to bear together. The storm had passed and we secured the cave in case we needed to return—if we could.

"I feel as though it's some kind of judgment for what our city has done."

"But what exactly have we done, Thomas?"

"Become monsters."

"I didn't feel that way, not in the midst of it anyway. I was just afraid."

"Why isn't it happening again?"

"It may be they're testing us. Seeing how we respond to different doses."

"Habituating us."

"Yes."

I couldn't see the crow, or any other bird. It seemed almost hot enough to melt the snow but it did not; we made our way slowly towards a rocky outcrop on the horizon towards which our compass pointed.

I thought about the crow, and his flight. The feeling of the air underneath my belly, and the sun in my face. I thought about my chicks back at home, and the years ahead. The sky was the color of ice, blue mixed with green, cold and shimmering with light. I wheeled in place above my tree, looking for the sign.

The sign spread out over the land, but its ligament was in this tree—one of its many tails. I looked to see where its hand might reveal itself, a white tongue in the light over the snow-dusted branches.

67.

There are no burial rites for me; likely I will be burned a heretic and my ashes scattered into the alleys of the slums of my city. Until that day arrives I am protected; I think they are waiting to see what I will say.

I could say that I look forward to the burning but this is not quite right. It is some sun who has invaded my darkness and about whom I must spin; penning the words I believe will keep him out of my bed.

Hold the thought inside your head:

I am better.

Whatever they have done does not mean I must also succumb to its forces; whatever deals they made are off.

Whatever demon they serve can be exorcised; if you will it. Want it. What I refuse to sacrifice in blood will then be taken in some other form:

Some little abstinence; a pause before judgment; the fate of the day brought closer in, opened up, a book, for you to read:

Write down your name inside it. Choose.

What is it you have come to do. Who do you pledge to your honor and what are they worth, in battle?

- -

What is it I've done—and who am I speaking to? What major arcana sleeps inside me, shifting my eyes to see these dreams. Which murder in me tightens inside my hands, rises in my neck, into my ears? I've returned—to my captors, to my slavers, my mendicant friars bonded to the workhorse of my country's false history—tell me what it is I should do.

The weight of the act itself—like that of electing a false king—is slight enough, but it grows with each day that passes, insisting that you did not know the full extent of it. This is your wave, man, now ride it, or it will smother you and all of your past.

What is it I've done, and what will you do,
friend, if I convince you that I am right, and
that your life depends on what I must tell you?

68.

I can feel it coming over me, Wenclas with me then, and now, alone—both at once. The black state of the body, and the rite over the sky, also dark, whose enveloping arms move me not only to write, and dream, but take my hands into these terrible events which I must narrate, if I have the strength.

Holocausts are, of course, whole burnings. The reduction into ash of the body, like the sky's light into darkness. That I may take part in them, even as I am their son, fills me with both joy and shame, that I should be a creature of this market for violence, scarred and ready to take my hand in arms to ply the names of my city and discover where they are buried.

Where did you bury the names? Father? I will turn every stone up out of the ground.

- -

The fear is its own friend, like gravity, or love. The kind of nearness whose presence shakes the mind into awareness and stretches over the eyes to reveal the shape of the world. Whose patience is it I am fearing? What kind of thing is it to kill your hopes, dreams, faith, winter and reason? Not suicide or birth. Switching back and forth between the lights who cover my mind and decision, whiteblack to blackwhite, and nearing still closer the nature of the thing—need.

I need the fear closer so I can know how deep it stretches; and which cords its limbic minorities and telegraphies resurrect in the act of vengeance.

"Are you there Wenclas?"

". . ."

"Tell me, are you there?"

"Thomas?"

"Are you all right?"

"You're still alive?"

"I'm coming back Wenclas. I'm going to kill Mr. Genevieve."

I put down the phone and stare out the window.

Perhaps these actions will be meaningless—ineffective, selfish, callous. But inaction is worse. I want to watch what it means to combat the leviathan.

Part 4

69.

We're not really here; or not near enough. The funny thing about mind control rays is, having discovered them, it rapidly becomes impossible to remove other categories of influence from this same ray—as though the act itself of observing the phenomenon opens a gravity well to suck in adjacent and similar phenomena until they become inseparable.

Of course it is impossible to oversimplify the world in any actual, physical way. Its complexity will always find ways under your tent. Challenges to any explanation, any theory.

Still we are not quite here: and I suspect we're coming closer.

"Wenclas, are you there?"

The sound of the white sky is like dreams.

"Wenclas?"

"Who is this?"

It's a woman's voice.

"Who is this?" I say into the receiver.

"I'm Wenclas' wife. Who is this?"

"His wife?"

"Is this his friend Thomas?"

"I want to speak to Wenclas."

"What year do you think it is, Thomas?"

I put down the receiver into the antique plastic cradle. Outside it has begun to snow again. How long have I been writing?

70.

What if we were done, and all our empires overthrown, and the rigid night air no longer cold; streets were swept and the lights in the distance came closer, dancing with us:

What is it to become again a living thing?

Out of the cancer and waste?

71.

I fear there is no escape but within. But what would it mean to escape inside? How could I exist, save as a kind of vegetable, if I retreat so fully from the borders of my self? It may be I have already been there; and that this world is already the retreat. We are already attached to the devices in the basement, reading out the logs of their transmissions.

Who should I cry to for help?

Thomas, is it you?

Angela.

Are you all right?

Yes, I'm fine.

What are you doing?

Where are you?

At the university.

What do you want?

I need to help you.

Why?

Because I got in trouble. Will you come back?

I am coming back. But I don't know if I can help you.

It's I who want to help you.

What are you willing to do?

I have some money.

It wouldn't be enough. I'll need a propagandist, and an assassin. Can you do that?

I don't know.

Where can I meet you?

At my place.

Somewhere public.

At the square.

I should be back by the weekend.

Be careful.

- -

I feel the connection break . . . I'm left in my house overlooking the fields. This nice government house.

72.

Who is it falling, falling over the shore, watching me come in to these waters, to drown? Fate me, fate me, should I insist on drinking these lands and die; to be inside:

'What is it you've been doing?'

'So many things, Thomas'

'I want to know'

'You can't'

'Won't you tell me? please'

'It's like you: this thing who is you, tempest-tossed and sulky in the mire and mud, a driftwood log homespun and waterlogged, unfeeling but still alive, sent over the ordure to find the lock and key you've been dreaming of in your sleep, for some door you will not understand . . .'

'I know, but tell me anyway, won't you?'

'I'll try . . .'

I'll hold her hand, the LadyThing of AllBright and Dead, numbering me among the canyons of her history, shaking and shriking the reeds and rebels with her work and words, all burials . . . all divinities cut like holes in the loam to make room for seeds:

'It's beautiful'

She says nothing, escorting me over the fallows to the antechamber of the wood, just some benches before the trees:

'You have a lot to do,' she says.

'I know.'

'Are you ready?'

'Will I die?' I ask.

'Yes,' she says.

73.

'What am I supposed to say?'

'Are you ready?'

"No. Yes.'

The spirit is not meant to be only in the body—
yet in its excursions, and in the rendering of
those excursions down, into the meal, ready
with ink, we find the ready reed and rill of
the world, cut down and censored, lifted with
smoke and silt: lift.

I am lifted; as she drives the knife into my back
and through my heart.

She is like a nature spirit—one of her forms.
And I am like the committee, borne in on the
work, to uncover the guilt inside the recesses
of the Citadel.

Patient and buried like saints I rise steadfast
over the wind to descend upon my cynosure,
the beady ball of wax—my Braunschweig. Her

hideous visage rises like a plague corpse over the steady wind, her towers effigies to the dark gods beneath.

I step into Angela's chamber. She has a lover in the bed.

I fill the room with my body: a ghost.

The man screams and runs to the door; she sits up in her bed, screaming.

A smile is on my face.

"Take me to Mr. Genevieve."

74.

It's not true to say whatsoever I learned before is gone; rather it is transmuted, under my flesh, into new shapes and stories.

My muse, who is a kind of shade over my head, summons me into Braunschweig's brain:

Hear me, muse, I who am light, shut up inside this ephemeral body, to enter my tone and trade into the sound of my former masters:

'What are you doing here, Thomas?'

"Mr. Genevieve," I say.

'You're too late. Whatever you thought you were going to do. The City is to remain asleep.'

'But Mr. Genevieve. All I want is vengeance.'

- -

That things should persevere, or rather cohere, despite my most violent imaginings, speaks perhaps to something like fate, still at work under our feet despite my every desire—who, after all, cares for my desires? These random patterns of pinecones dropping onto the tin roof in a rainstorm. That the shape of the world becomes not hazier but clearer—that I should still, and in spite of my repeated failures, be coming closer to an understanding of the operations of my world—fills me inexplicably with regret. Perhaps I came to Braunschweig to forget, and am disappointed that the journey instead has been one of discovery.

The shape of my will itself—so alike in death and life—fires warm around my soul, a weather pattern harmonically fused to the workings of my mind, my desires, deeper and broader now that I have parted from the required course of my study.

Who was it pulled the wool over our eyes?

And why did we permit it to happen?

75.

We imagine—or I do—that we know the limits
of life and death, when one passes into another.
We suppose, often, that the time of miracles is
either long past, or that they never were—mere
myths. Yet both myths and miracles come from
the same source: for our ancestors, myth was
"mouth" and miracle was "smile." The things
we do with this strange little toothy organ.

Did not Orpheus go down to Hades and re-
trieve Eurydice from beyond oblivion? Though
at great cost. And I who have been nothing but
a slave, even in my adventures beyond the city
you know, remained so in my coming to face
with that woman beyond the grave who granted me this spirit-life, and then returned me to
my body.

We should grant some space in the narrative
for miracles. I imagine no voice of God—I am
he, and only a small thing. Rather let it be the
sound of rain.

Each droplet and its accompanying ecosystem

forms around a granule of bacteria, drifting inside the sky, looking for a ticket back to earth.

I am the ticket, coalescing slow as water into the air, and the eyes of the germs, infinitesimal but not exactly infinite, gorge my senses to their flow and waist, like the waist of a woman, adhering only to the rhythm of her step.

I cut open his throat and watch the blood poor onto the floor.

76.

I put on his clothes and run down his spiral stairs, robes swishing around my feet. I feel good for the first time in a long time; it must be the killing. I reach the Council Room, wires hanging out of the walls, where I awoke to see Angela in what seems some prior lifetime— which I suppose is what it was.

Mr. Genevieve's sigil is still in his pocket, its shape like the spiral which we danced. Almost I hear his voice in my head, whispering obscene things. His body not yet cold. I press the metal against the slot in the door and enter his private sanctum, the upload link to the mothership.

I know these things because of my departure and return—both from Braunschweig and from this life. The blue lights of the panels look submarine, shimmering over my face. I raise the microphone to my mouth from the console.

"Hello?"

77.

Who are you to take me so freely, underneath your sleeve, bow and scrape and steely-eyed escort me underneath the barge of your undying regard, so deep and stretching far it seems eternal? I thought I had you in my sight when I was young; I thought I breathed you, smelled you, took you into my mouth, like a strand of my hair, to see just what it tasted like—tell me what the barrier wall is and how you made it!

Tell me the reason for your terrible silences! Tell me the name of the ocean you spawned from! It can't have been ours.

All this I wanted to say. But all that came out of my mouth when I heard their voice was

"Uhhhhhhh—

78.

What kind of burr is it, love, eating you alive?
No man can survive it—even in death it haunts
you, stomping against your memories and lives,
insisting that the blood you spilled—your own
and others—was only incidental to the spines
of its attachment to your body, ghostly or otherwise, standing or sleeping or dead.

Angela had attached herself to the wall to die,
running one of the torture programs the brothers had been developing. Her sweat-covered
flesh twitched against the grey stone, blooding
pouring from her mouth.

I tore the wires out of her head and kissed her;
her eyes opened but saw nothing. I reached
into her heart and squeezed it into life, and
some dark radiance came over her face then—
part of my ghost.

"You revived me," she said.

"I don't know."

"You did."

"No."

"I know you did."

"I'm already dead."

"Help me get dressed."

I wiped the blood off her skin with a sponge and held her robe for her. She smiled at me—a ghost of her former smile.

"Why did you want to die?" I asked.

"Let's go up to the roof," she said.

The snow was coming down in red waves, marching over the legions of the continent, this space I must leave too soon. Snow the color of blood.

"This was why," she said.

"I'm sorry I revived you," I said.

"Why did you do it?"

"For love."

"The stupidest reason!"

I held onto her hand.

"What's happened to us?" I said. "Are we in hell?"

"I don't know."

It was strangely beautiful, like watching a mold grow in time lapse over a rock, the surfaces of my city turned a bright crimson.

"I think I'm a ghost," I said.

"Can't you kill me again?" she said.

"No."

I walked down the stairs out into the nightmare. I had forgotten my dog. Perhaps my greatest sin. He wasn't in the apartment. I called Wen-clas.

"Do you have Henry?"

"Thomas?"

"Is Henry okay?"

"Yes. He's fine."

"Are you at your place?"

"Yes, at my house. But you shouldn't come now. Something is happening. Look up, man."

"I know. This snow. Our friends are coming."

79.

Carry me over the river; I can see the light.
Broadbacked on either side, an ocean of light,
transmitted in a frequency I can understand.
Red yellow light spread over the bank, on my
hands and cheeks, like turmeric. What I can see
is the shape of it; like weights carrying one
deep beneath the sea, I feel the sky shift overhead, marring the great radiance of the heavens with the shift of its lens, door wafting in
the breeze:

Overhead, the ships are arriving.

\- -

The dear end shakes the sound of the town
doll in rage
tearing the seams:

Not every chapter is finished.
I have some of the words in my drawer.
Rattling against the wood.

who made the nation so silent?

the tomb of some evil regret.
was it you?

I can see your face, like a guard's,
watching the sky for the coming dark.

80.

There are no deaths left; I have spent them all.
I am stuck with life. I escaped the prison of
university but not the prison of love.

81.

Come down into the dark with me, and I'll show you something different from the bitter wind, curling over the faces of Braunschweig's growing towers, or the night who waits below, curling around your feet;   I'll show you how death comes into you, and by which door.

He enters in secret, for he has been invited, into the tunnels. Where he may run below, to the appointed place, for his meeting. Where all of the night waits for him.

Come with me, if you would see me end—I must do it; I want to desperately. Do it with me, you who are like me in the wildered fluid of this world, so I will know I have been seen in death, more beautiful than I was in life, centered and surrounded in the knowledge of this keep, who is a piece of my heart.

This keep is a piece of Braunschweig, held below with all the other secrets: memories, maps, potions, passwords, keys, and some of the weapons our predecessors used before they came here. All of these old things.

Come down into the dark with me, won't you?
To know how it feels when the light is gone,
and the serpent has wrapped his face around
the towers, and all that is left is to see the last
light fade from the sky,

Be the last light for me, as I go below.

82.

The winter of the night is upon me, like a dark ray come to steal my will, pressing me into the cockpit beneath the wings of the city. Braun-schweig was never home to me but I found I loved it, once it was no longer my own.

The towers slip beneath the fog; the last red lights marking their growing tips spreading out like into the darkening night; glimmering fire.

I'm going through the roof of the dome; to all that lies above. All around me the dark wings of the ship shimmer, like subterranean waters. The craft obeys commands I hold inside my head.

Henry is in my lap. Outside, the sky opens like a door. The dog is unafraid; but I am. I close my eyes and we slip through into the dark above.

About the author

Robin Wyatt Dunn was born in Wyoming in 1979. You can read more of his work at www.robindunn.com.